To my darling Lily. You are my inspiration and
my favorite collaborator. I'm lucky to be your dad.

First published in 2020 by Dial Books for Young Readers,
an imprint of Penguin Random House LLC, New York

First published in Great Britain 2020 by Egmont Books UK Ltd
2 Minster Court, London EC3R 7BB
www.egmontbooks.co.uk

EGMONT
We bring stories to life

Text and illustration copyright © Michael Slack 2020
The moral rights of Michael Slack have been asserted.

ISBN 978 07555 0003 1

71300/001

A CIP catalogue record for this book is available from the British Library.

KITTENS ON DINOSAURS

Michael Slack

EGMONT

Well, kittens. You are officially expert climbers.

You've climbed everything there is to climb.

Your cat tree. ☑

A real tree. ☑

An ancient litter box in the trees. ☑

Now what?

The dinosaurs on Dinosaur Island?

Kittens, that's **bonkers!**

You are cuddly. You are cute.
They are humongous. They will eat you alive.

You do **not want** to climb those dinosaurs.

Too late.

You are determined to climb the dinosaurs.

Don't do it, kittens. They look hungry.

Uh-oh. They've spotted you.
Now you're in trouble.

Good idea. Get in your litter mobile and sail back to Kitten Island.

Fast!

SCRATCH SCRATCH

SCRATCH

TAP

TAP

TAP

Um . . . what are you doing in there, kittens?

Close call, furballs.
You barely escaped.

Let me guess. Plan C?

PLAN C:
Cat-mouflage

Well, kittens. You did your best. You tried hard, but . . .

No one **ever** has a plan D.

Tough cookies, kittens. Your plans didn't work. Time to accept defeat.

I'm going to miss you all.

Wow. I did NOT see this coming.

Even prehistoric grumpy lizards can't resist
your cuddly cuteness.

You did it, kittens! Your plan D actually worked. I was wrong. I was 100% certain you would be eaten alive.

Now you've really climbed everything there is to climb.

Dinosaurs on Dinosaur Island.

Umm . . .

. . . scratch that.

You've climbed the **tiny baby** dinosaurs on Dinosaur Island whose mummies have been looking for them.

Kittens. Don't even **think** about climbing the Mummysaurs!

Too late.

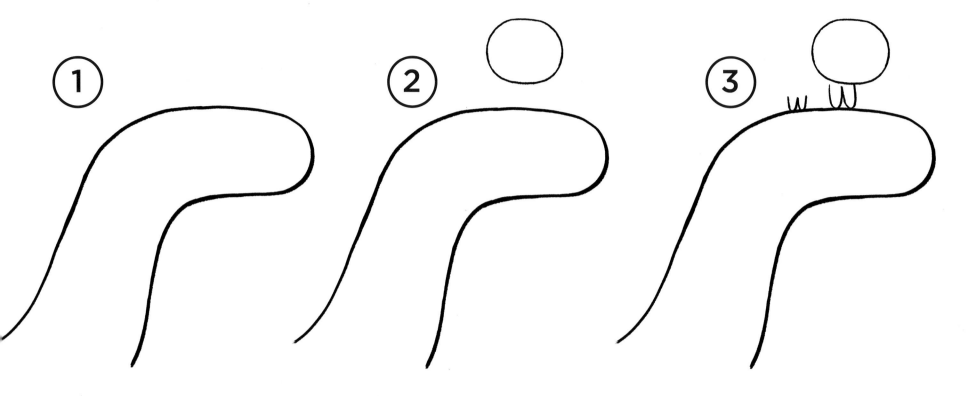

How to draw a

KITTEN ON A DINOSAUR

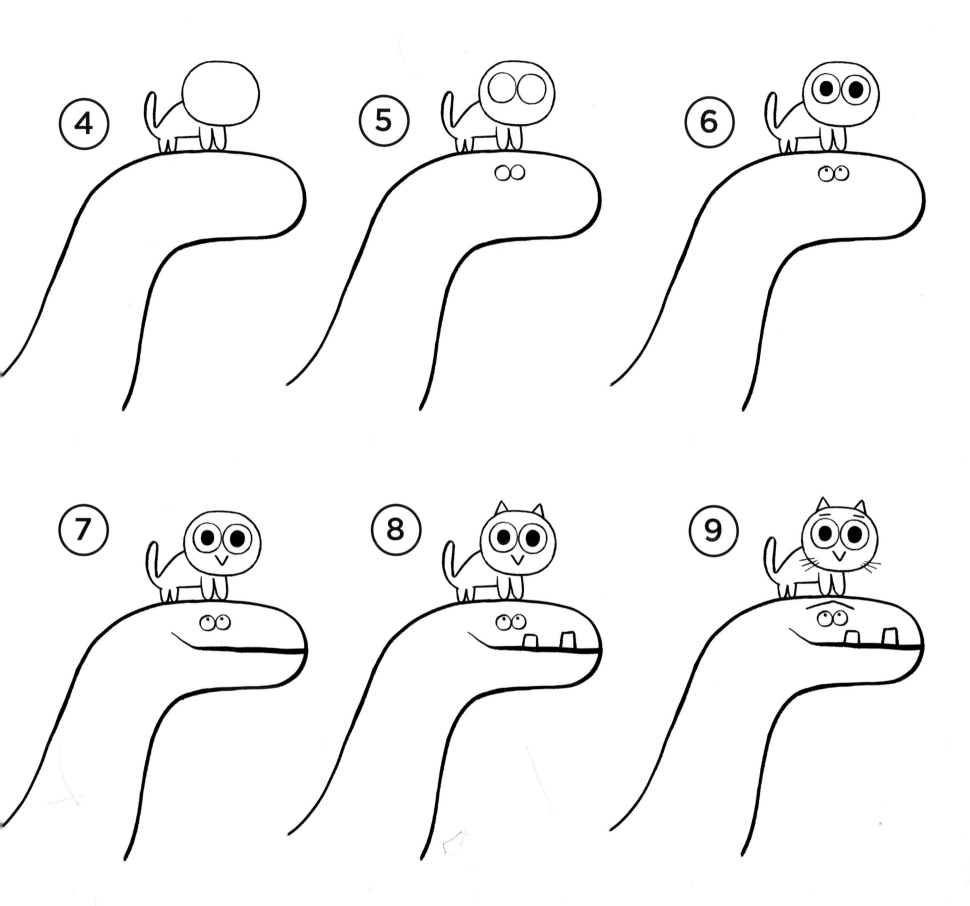

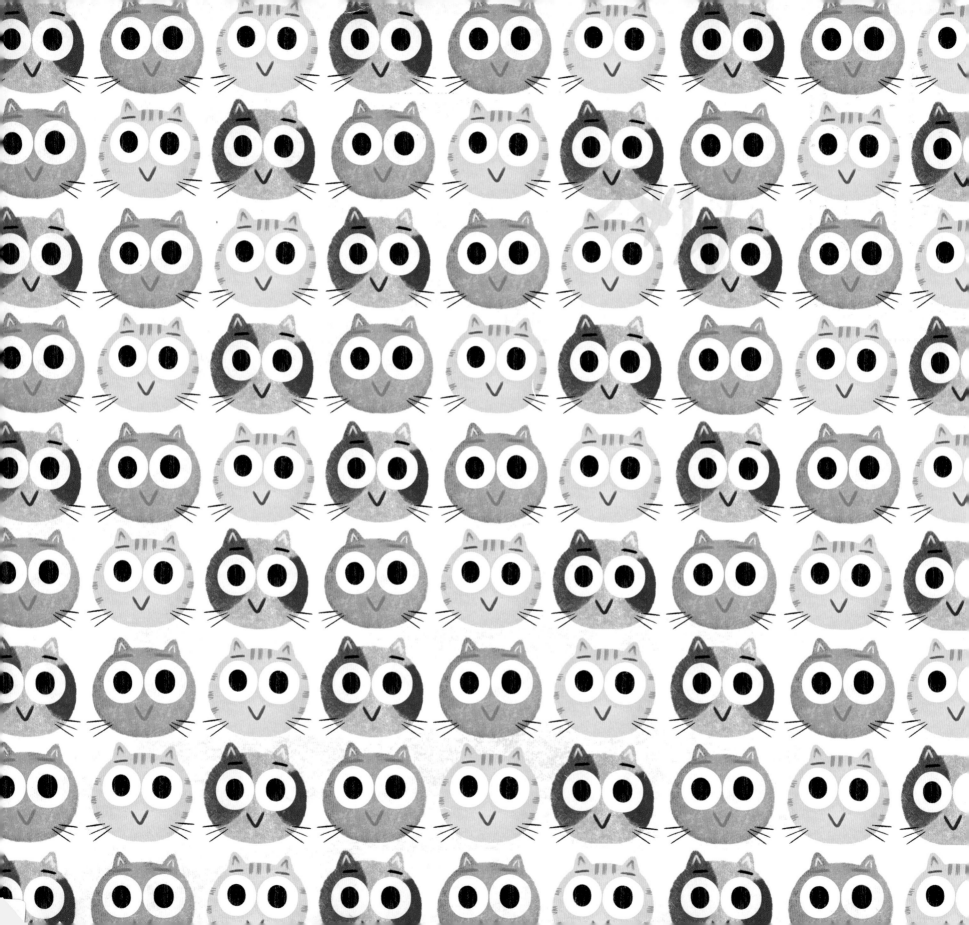